House
Finds
a Home

By

KATY S. DUFFIELD

Illustrated by

JEN CORACE

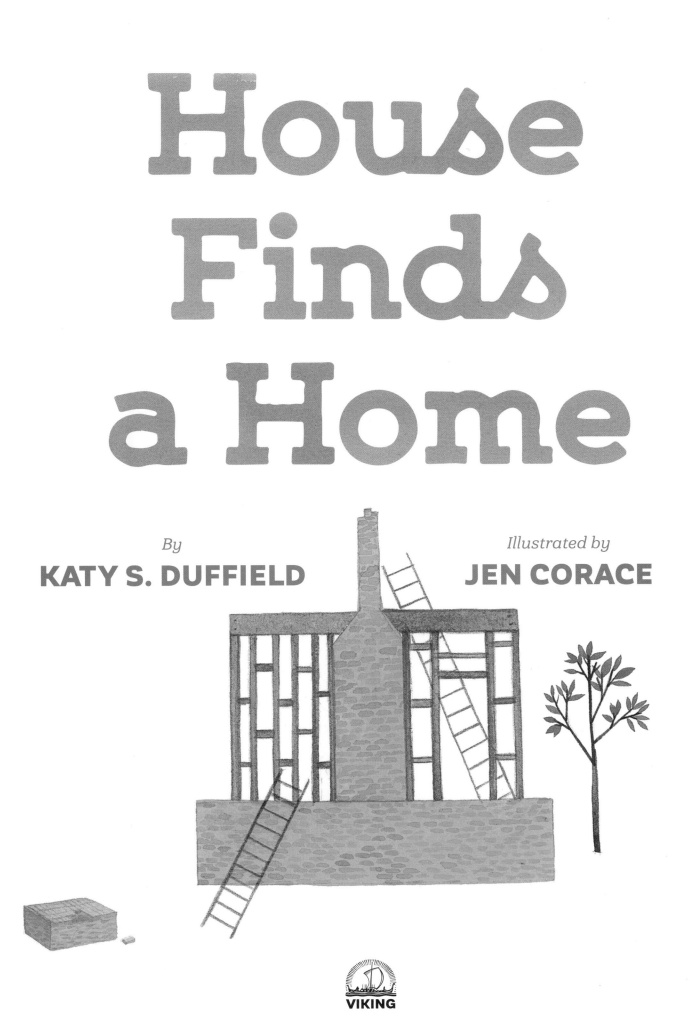

VIKING

You might think
houses don't have hearts.
But House had one.
And it was broken.

Over the years, House and his people
had made a mountain of memories—

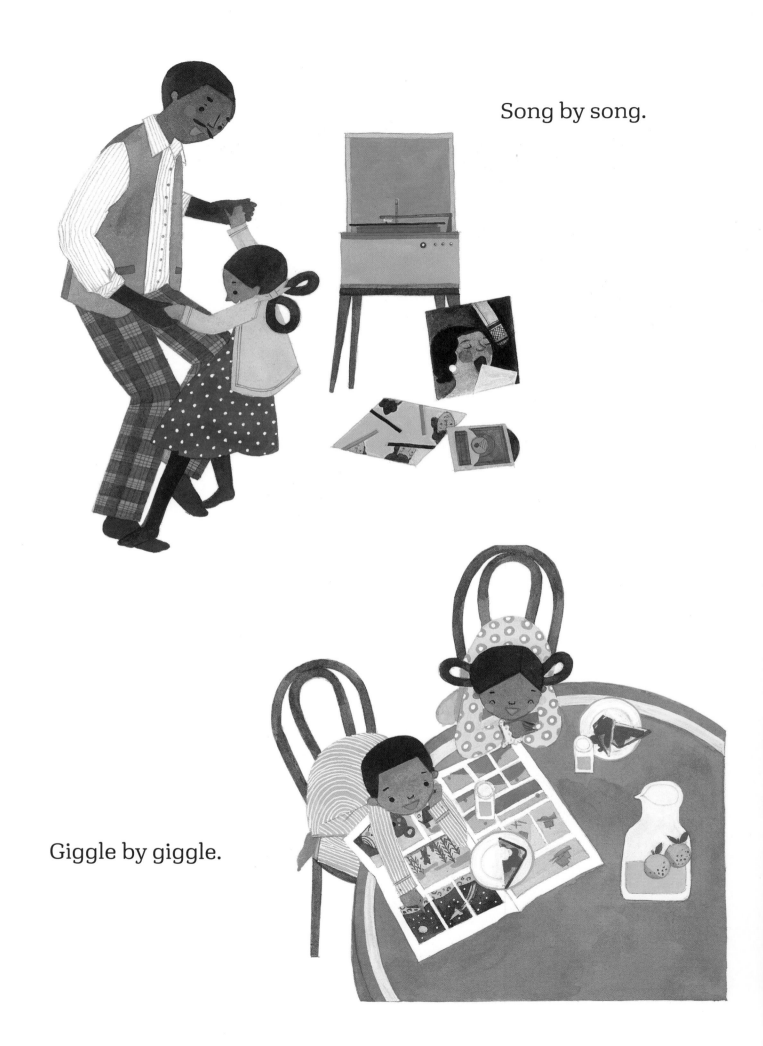

Song by song.

Giggle by giggle.

Hug by hug.

But House's people had
new memories to make.
And House's once-full heart
was now as empty as his rooms.

House was quiet for a while.

Dark.

But then . . .

. . . something happened.

Visitors climbed his front porch steps,
oohed over his sturdy brick,
aahed over his cozy rooms.
And after a while, new people moved in!

They made House
their home, their way.

And for months—years, even—
House's heart was happy.

Until . . .
House's halls grew quiet,
his windows dark—once again.

House hoped.
Hoped with all his shingles—

And his wishes came true!
The new people made House
their home, their way.

And for months—years, even—
House's heart was happy.

But—
life changes.

And House found himself alone once again.

House didn't let himself fall
into disrepair though.
Because, as the years had tumbled by,
House had learned something:

when one door closes, another door opens . . .

And each and every time, through those doors,
House found what he'd been missing—love.

And on this day, when love clambered in,
House noticed something familiar.

Something oh so familiar.

House and his new family began making
a new mountain of memories—
song by song.

Giggle by giggle.

Hug by hug.

It wasn't always
perfect . . .

But it was better
than fine.

MUCH better than fine.

In fact . . . it was as fine
as fine could get.

You might think houses
don't have hearts.
But House had one.

And House's once-full
heart wasn't just full again . . .
it was overflowing.

For Dad, Mom, Julie, Andy, and 1519.
—K.D.

To my home that has housed me for
nearly ten years and all the evidence of
the people who lived here before me.
—J.C.

VIKING
An imprint of Penguin Random House LLC, New York

First published in the United States of America by Viking,
an imprint of Penguin Random House LLC, 2022

Visit us online at penguinrandomhouse.com.

Library of Congress Cataloging-in-Publication Data is available.

Manufactured in China

ISBN 9780593204603

1 3 5 7 9 10 8 6 4 2

TOPL

Design by Jim Hoover   Text set in Australis Pro
The illustrations for this book were made with gouache, ink, and pencil on Rives BFK.